# How to Work the Monster's Ring

To change yourself into a hideous monster, place the
ring on the ring finger of your right hand. Grasp it with
your left hand. Turn the ring to the left. The strength of
the spell depends on how many twists you give the ring:

Twist it once, you're horned and haired;
Twist it twice and fangs are bared;
Twist it thrice? No one has dared!

Use with caution, *and never on the night of a full moon.*
To return to normal, turn the ring to the right.

Have fun!

**Books by Bruce Coville**

*Camp Haunted Hills*:
    How I Survived My Summer Vacation
    Some of My Best Friends Are Monsters
    The Dinosaur That Followed Me Home

*Magic Shop Books*:
    Jennifer Murdley's Toad
    Jeremy Thatcher, Dragon Hatcher
    The Monster's Ring

*My Teacher Books*:
    My Teacher Is an Alien
    My Teacher Fried My Brains
    My Teacher Glows in the Dark
    My Teacher Flunked the Planet

Goblins in the Castle

Monster of the Year

Space Brat

Available from MINSTREL® Books

# THE MONSTER'S RING

## BRUCE COVILLE

### illustrated by
### KATHERINE COVILLE

A MINSTREL® BOOK

PUBLISHED BY POCKET BOOKS

New York   London   Toronto   Sydney   Tokyo   Singapore

## TO ORION

This novel is a work of fiction. Names, characters, places and incidents are either the product of the author's imagination or are used fictitiously. Any resemblance to actual events or locales or persons, living or dead, is entirely coincidental.

A Minstrel Book published by
POCKET BOOKS, a division of Simon & Schuster, Inc.,
1230 Avenue of the Americas, New York, N.Y. 10020

Text copyright © 1982 by Bruce Coville
Illustrations copyright © 1982 by Katherine Coville
Cover artwork copyright © 1987 by Barclay Shaw

Published by arrangement with Pantheon Books,
a division of Random House, Inc.
Library of Congress Catalog Card Number: 82-3436

ISBN: 0-671-69389-1

First Minstrel Books printing October, 1987

10   9   8   7

A MINSTREL BOOK and colophon are trademarks of Simon & Schuster, Inc.

Printed in the U.S.A.

# Contents

# THE
# MONSTER'S
# RING

# ONE

# The Magic Shop

Russell Crannaker looked up and down the alley.

It was empty.

Perfect. He could practice in peace.

Putting up his arms, Russell staggered forward. He rolled back his eyes so only the whites were showing and began to moan.

Fantastic! He was going to be great as Frankenstein's monster—the best ever.

Russell relaxed and grinned. Halloween should be all right this year after all.

He moaned and lurched forward again. *Franken-stein.* Boy, would he love to *be* Frankenstein for a while. Then he'd show that Eddie a thing or two. He could see it now—Eddie kneeling in front of him, whining, pleading for mercy.

He could even hear Eddie's voice. "Please, Russell. Please don't hurt me. Please. *Please!*"

Russell smiled. It was a pleasant daydream. But his smile quickly turned to a frown. Something was wrong. Eddie was still talking!

"Oh, no! Save me, save me! It's the horrible Crankenstein! Hey, Crannaker, what's up? You lose your marbles?"

Russell opened his eyes and turned pale. There was Eddie, standing at the mouth of the alley.

"Come here, creep," sneered Eddie. "I'll make you *really* look like Frankenstein."

Russell started to shake. So far that day Eddie had tripped him, punched him, and smashed him in the face with a cream-filled cupcake. Under the circumstances only one thing made sense. Russell did it. He turned and ran.

"Hey, Crannaker! Whassa matter? You afraid?"

Afraid? Of course he was afraid! Lately he had lived in fear of what Eddie might do next.

He rounded the back corner of the alley and tripped over a row of garbage cans. One fell, spreading trash from wall to wall. Eddie shot around the corner after him, struck something slimy, and slid to his seat.

"I've got to get out of here," Russell thought. "Got to get away . . . now!" He was off like a shot.

He was on some back street. Without thinking, without looking, he ran. He came to another corner, made another right. Suddenly everything was quiet.

He stopped. Where was Eddie?

4

He looked around.

To his surprise, he was alone. Not only that, he was on a street that was completely new to him. That bothered him a little. But it was no real problem. He knew Kennituck Falls fairly well. He couldn't be far from a main street.

He walked to the next corner, figuring that would take him back to where he had started. It didn't. He turned right again—and then again. He was confused now. And scared. Not scared the way he had been when Eddie was after him. He was scared because *Kennituck Falls was too small to get lost in.* . . .

It was starting to get dark. A fog began to rise, the mist curling up and clutching at his feet.

Russell stopped again. He had reached a dead-end street. The shops lining its sides were closed. Except one. Directly ahead of him, a light burning in its window, there crouched a store that took his breath away. The sign in the window read:

ELIVES' MAGIC SUPPLIES
S. H. ELIVES, PROP.

Russell sighed. He was always crazy about magic, but in October he was consumed with a desire to experience it. His worries about being lost disappeared. He *had* to see what was in that shop!

He hurried forward. Through a window dark with the grime of years, he could see a crammed display of typical magicians' stock—cards, top hats, and so on.

But there was more here—dark boxes with mysterious designs, capes with dragons on them, a skull with a candle on its top. . . .

He loved it.

He opened the door. Overhead a small bell tinkled once.

But the shop was empty. There was no one in sight, not even a clerk.

Russell didn't care. He was too thrilled by the shop. It was jam-packed, from top to botton, with magic equipment. There was even a section of live animals—doves and rabbits, mostly, for pulling out of hats, but also lizards, toads, and snakes!

Russell heard a sound. He turned. The stuffed owl sitting on the cash register looked at him, blinked once, and hooted.

Russell froze.

That was when the old man appeared behind the counter.

Old?

Ancient was more like it. His withered brown skin reminded Russell of dried mushrooms. He was shorter than Russell, and probably weighed less. Yet for some reason he seemed very, very strong.

It might have been the eyes that glittered like black diamonds below his bristling brow.

He put a hand on the owl's head. "What is it, Uwila?"

His voice was like dead leaves rustling in an autumn wind.

The owl turned and stared at Russell. The old man's gaze followed. His eyes widened and flashed for a second, as if he were surprised to see the boy.

"What do you need?"

Russell shivered. "I . . . I just came in to look," he stammered.

"No one comes *here* just to look. Get to the point. What do you need?"

"Honestly, sir—I just came in to see what you have."

The old man arched one eyebrow and squinted his other eye shut. "Well, you've seen it. Now—what do you need?"

The tone of his voice made it clear to Russell that he had better need something. He looked around desperately. There were no price tags in sight. Fishing in his pocket, he found a crumpled bill—lunch money he had saved by being too nervous to eat.

"I only have a dollar," said Russell, "and . . ."

"That's enough!" snapped the old man. He stepped forward and snatched the money from Russell. "I have what you need. Stay here while I get it."

Russell stayed. He couldn't have moved if he had tried.

After what seemed like hours the old man reappeared, carrying a small black box.

"Here," he said. "Take this. *It's what you came for.*"

Russell's fingers trembled as he took the package.

"Now for Ishtar's sake," hissed the old man—and

his voice dropped to such a frightening whisper that Russell felt as though a cold wind had run down his spine—"*be careful!*"

Russell looked around wildly. It was very dark.

"Take that door," said the old man. "It will get you home faster."

He began to laugh.

Russell spotted the small door at the side of the shop and bolted for it as though the Hounds of Hell were at his heels. Outside he continued to run, without looking where he was going, until he could go no farther. Then he stopped, panting, and leaned against a wall.

Looking up, he found to his surprise that he was back in the alley where he had started. He wondered if it had all been a dream.

Then he remembered the package in his hand. That was real enough.

What had he bought, anyway?

He looked at the box. Across the top, in flaming red letters, it said . . . THE MONSTER'S RING.

# TWO

# With a Twist of the Ring...

Russell smiled. He was very fond of monsters. (In fact, he had the largest collection of monster magazines of anyone in the fifth grade.)

Using his fingernail, he slit the tape that held the box shut.

Inside the box was a ring. It was made of cheap metal. But set in its top was a green stone carved with a monster's face. Delighted, Russell took it out and slipped it onto his finger.

A sudden chill ran through his body. He shook his head and shivered.

There was a neatly folded piece of paper in the bottom of the box. He took it out and opened it.

At the top of the page was a picture of the monster, its arms spread across the page, its face leering.

Below that were the words, "How to Work the Monster's Ring."

Work it? How could you "work" a ring?

He read on.

"To change yourself into a hideous monster, place the ring on the ring finger of your right hand. Grasp it with your left hand. Turn the ring to the left as you repeat this chant. . . ."

"To change yourself into a hideous monster"— what junk! He had sworn off that kind of thing after he got those useless "X-ray Specs" from the back of a *Muck Critter* comic.

Russell crumpled the paper in disgust, crammed it into his pocket, and headed for home.

"Where have you been, Russell?" asked his mother when he walked through the door.

"Oh, just messing around."

"Well, get cleaned up. It's almost time for supper."

Supper was a typical Crannaker family meal. His mother fussed over him as he ate, his father talked on and on (and *on*!), and Russell sat chasing peas around mashed potato mountains with his fork.

He was considering telling his parents about the problems he was having with Eddie. But his father had gotten going on one of his pet theories, something about the future of civilization, and he wouldn't run down for hours.

Russell loved his father, but trying to get a word in edgewise when he was talking was like trying to stop a freight train by standing in front of it: you were bound to get run down. So Russell simply tuned out.

Fortunately Mr. Crannaker didn't seem to care if anyone listened to him or not. As long as he was talking, he was happy.

"Eat your pork chop, dear," said Russell's mother when his father stopped to chew.

Russell looked down at his plate and grimaced.

The night wore on, and Russell forgot about the ring until bedtime, when it caught on his shirt as he was undressing. He grinned. That monster *was* neat. Just for the fun of it, he took out the directions and spread them on his dresser top. Then he began to twist the ring while he whispered the chant from the top of the page:

"Powers Dark and Powers Bright,
I call you now, as is my right.
Unleash the magic of this ring
And change me to a monstrous thing!"

He waited, feeling very silly.

Nothing happened.

"X-ray Specs," he said, and shrugged. He headed for the bathroom to wash up, more disappointed than he cared to admit.

Halfway down the hall Russell got a strange feeling in his forehead, as if something was trying to break through the skin. It didn't hurt. It was just . . . weird.

He put his hand on his brow and felt something sharp and hard. He tried to pull it off. No luck.

He ran to the bathroom, looked in the mirror, and nearly fainted.

He had horns!

He had horns coming out of his forehead—horns an inch long, and getting longer.

Mouth agape, Russell watched the transformation. Suddenly hair began to sprout from his face. He needed a shave.

Shave? He needed a lawn mower!

He touched the horns. They seemed to have stopped growing. But they were almost three inches long now, and *very* sharp.

Russell looked in the mirror again. Beneath the horns his brows met in a single shaggy line that ran straight across his forehead. Beneath that line flashed two yellow eyes, holding a strange hint of inner fire. His nose—flatter than an old prizefighter's—was nearly lost in the thick beard that hid his neck and chin.

The backs of his hands were covered with curling black fur.

He wanted to scream. No—that would only bring his parents.

Suddenly he realized that even though he was frightened, he was also excited. Strange as it was, this was the most *interesting* thing that had ever happened to him.

He looked in the mirror and snarled. It made him jump. He tried it again.

"Boy, would that ever do a number on Eddie."

He chuckled at the idea, sounding like an angry bear.

This was ridiculous. He was dreaming. He pinched himself to prove it.

Unfortunately his fingernails were now deadly claws. He drew blood, and the sharp pain convinced him that he was indeed awake.

Panic set in.

How long would this last?

He opened the bathroom door and peered out. Good. His parents were still downstairs. He stepped out and headed for his room—and the directions.

Without intending to, he stomped all the way down the hall.

"Russell, is that you?"

It was his mother.

He froze.

"Russell?"

He strained to make his voice seem normal. "Yes, Mom. I was just going to bed. Good night."

He sounded like he had been gargling with razor blades.

"Are you all right, Russell? You sound a little hoarse."

"No! I'm fine! Just got a little frog in my throat."

"All right. But if it's not gone in the morning, I'm taking your temperature. And no arguments."

"Yes, Mother."

He collapsed against the wall.

Well, that was over. Now what?

He had to look at those directions!

He stepped into his room. But the moon was staring through his window. It caught his eye and drew him on.

He crossed to the sill.

The moon was *calling* him.

And deep within his monsterish breast something stirred in answer, something that insisted he could stay inside no longer.

Putting a paw on the sill, Russell vaulted over, and out, and into the night below.

A monster was loose in Kennituck Falls.

# THREE

# The Battle in the Cafeteria

Russell bounded joyfully out of bed. What a fantastic dream!

Suddenly he stopped dead in his tracks.

There were hairy feet sticking out of his pajamas.

He sat down.

Slowly.

So it wasn't a dream.

He shook his head as images began to flicker through his mind. He saw himself—his monster self—in action: growling at late shoppers, swinging on streetlamps, and—his cheeks burned at the memory—chasing cars down Main Street.

On all fours.

Snapping at the hubcaps!

Cripes. This was embarrassing.

He groaned as he remembered what had come next. Even now he wasn't sure how he had escaped from all those policemen.

It was a good thing his monster legs could move so fast.

He shuddered.

So he had made it back to his room somehow.

Wonderful.

*Now what?*

"Russell! Time for breakfast!"

His mother's voice doubled his panic. How could he go down there like this? What could he say? "Morning, Mom. Morning, Dad. What's wrong? Oh, *this*. Yes, it is a little weird, isn't it. . . ."

No, that would never do.

He stood up to pace the room and spotted a paper on his dresser.

The directions! What a dope! How could he have forgotten them? Being a monster must have addled his brains. He snatched up the paper.

There it was, in black and white—the antidote.

He sighed. His mother had told him time and again, "Read all the directions before you start a project."

Score one for Mom.

He examined the paper carefully. This time he read every word:

# HOW TO WORK THE MONSTER'S RING

To change yourself into a hideous monster, place the ring on the ring finger of your right hand. Grasp it with your left hand. Turn the ring to the left as you repeat this chant:

> Powers Dark and Powers Bright,
> I call you now, as is my right.
> Unleash the magic of this ring
> And change me to a monstrous thing!

The strength of the spell depends on how many twists you give the ring:

> Twist it once, you're horned and haired;
> Twist it twice and fangs are bared;
> Twist it thrice? No one has dared!

Use with caution, *and never on the night of a full moon*. To return to normal, turn the ring to the right, repeating this chant:

> Powers Bright and Powers Dark,
> Hark to one who bears your mark.
> Let now my shape return to me
> And make me as I used to be!

### HAVE FUN!

Trembling, Russell took the ring in his claws and twisted it as he repeated the final verse.

It worked! He could feel his horns beginning to shrink, his hair growing shorter, his claws turning back into nails. He wanted to shout for joy.

Then something occurred to him—a thought his panic had blinded him to before. If he had an antidote, *he could become a monster anytime he wanted.*

He began to laugh.

Russell was sitting in the cafeteria. School had been fun so far. The place was buzzing with rumors about the "maniac" that had run amok in town last night. It was all Russell could do to keep a straight face every time he heard one.

Missy Freebaker sat down next to him. "Did you hear about the monster, Russell? Isn't it scary?"

"I think it's silly," he said. "There's no such thing."

"Well, how come so many people saw it?"

"Maybe they were hallucinating."

She scowled. Russell smiled and turned to his lunch.

Then Eddie sat down opposite him.

Russell groaned as he felt a familiar lump form in his stomach. There was no doubt that Eddie would do something rotten. So there was no sense in even trying to eat. It wasn't worth the effort.

He looked up. Eddie was grinning at him, with all his teeth showing. Russell knew that grin well. It was a very bad sign.

There was a crash as someone on the other side of the cafeteria dropped a tray. Russell turned to look. When he turned back, Eddie was pouring chocolate milk all over his lunch.

Russell got angry. Then he got scared because he was angry. Then the anger became more important again.

He picked up his spoon and smacked Eddie's hand.

"What do you think you're doing, Crannaker?" screamed Eddie. He shoved Russell's tray so that it smashed into his chest.

Without thinking, Russell took what was left of his milk and threw it at Eddie. The carton struck his head, and chocolate milk poured over his face. Eddie howled. Lunging across the table, he grabbed Russell's shirt, shouting about how Russell was going to be sorry he was born, and how they were going to need a spatula to get him off the cafeteria walls.

Russell was crying. But he was also smacking Eddie on the head with his spoon, shouting "Stop it, stip ot, stoop it."

Eddie didn't stop.

Russell picked up his plate and dumped it on Eddie's head.

Spaghetti flew in all directions.

Eddie screeched. Russell saw strings of spaghetti hanging over his enemy's ears like some strange new hairdo and suddenly realized what he had done.

He was terrified.

Suddenly a hand grabbed Russell by the shoulder.

He was snapped around and found himself face to face with his teacher, Miss Snergal.

"*What is going on here?*" she cried. She was so angry she was shaking.

Russell and Eddie both started talking.

"Be quiet!" she snapped. She marched them out of the cafeteria. "You go wash up," she said to Eddie. "Russell, you wait here until I come for you. After lunch we'll make a little trip to the principal's office." She stood him beside the door and disappeared into the cafeteria.

Russell slid to the floor. The principal! He shuddered. Old Man Rafschnitz was the most feared person at Boardman Road Elementary School. Kids turned white at the mention of his name. And now he, Russell, had broken the rules.

He was being sent to *that* office.

He would have to face . . . "The Beast of Boardman Road."

He thought he was going to be sick.

Just then Eddie came swaggering back from the bathroom. He still had spaghetti sauce in his ears, but he was smirking as if he owned the world. He leaned against the door and smiled fiendishly down at Russell.

"Wait till school's over, Crannaker," he said. "I'm gonna mop up the hallways with you."

Russell began to tremble. Clasping his hands together to stop them from shaking, he felt the ring.

The ring!

A smile flickered over his face.

"Try it, bozo. See what happens."

The look on Eddie's face was perfect. He couldn't believe Russell would dare talk to him like that.

Russell began to chuckle. He couldn't believe it either. He, Russell, the meek and mild, making tough Eddie squirm.

He laughed out loud.

As he did so, Miss Snergal stepped back out of the cafeteria. "I don't see what's so funny, Mr. Crannaker," she said. "I had hoped that by now you would have realized the seriousness of what you've done."

"Oh yes, ma'am," said Russell. He scrambled to his feet, meek and mild again. "I do. Oh, do I ever!"

FOUR

# Russell vs. His Father's Mouth

Mr. Rafschnitz's face was beet red, and his nostrils flared out like a horse's. Just the sight of him was enough to turn Russell into jelly. He had a horrible feeling that he was going to melt and slide right off the chair.

"Well," growled Mr. Rafschnitz, "what do you have to say for yourself?"

There was a silence while Russell tried to think of an answer. But before he could come up with one, Mr. Rafschnitz began to pound his desk so hard that all the drawers in the filing cabinet rattled.

"Never mind the excuses!" he cried. "I hear excuses all day long. What I want to know is what we're going to do about this. Well, I'll *tell* you what we're going to do, Crannaker. We're going to keep an eye on you.

We're going to watch every move you make. One false step—*one teeny tiny move in the wrong direction*—*and* YOU'VE HAD IT!"

The roaring was giving Russell a headache. He looked down at the floor and nearly choked on the boulder growing in his stomach.

"I'm pleased to see you're properly ashamed," gloated Mr. Rafschnitz. "I have called your father. He will pick you up after school. He will, I'm sure, have much to say to you."

The boulder pushed Russell's stomach down to the bottom of his shoes and squashed it.

Mr. Rafschnitz was right. Russell's father had plenty to say to him. And he had been saying it from the moment Russell got into the car.

Now Russell was having a frightening thought. He was thinking he might try to make his father listen to him. It seemed impossible. But his father had been babbling on for ten minutes already, and Russell thought he was going to explode. He felt like he had swallowed a stick of dynamite—and his father's words were like matches, dropping near the fuse.

"I know life can be tough," his father was saying. "But violence isn't the answer. You know that. Violence is the tactic of ignorant . . ."

Russell tried it. "But Dad . . ."

The flow of words rushed over Russell like steam-roller. His father was unaware he had even *tried* to say anything.

"Now, this kind of behavior is not what your mother and I expect from you. You've been raised to know that dumping spaghetti on people's heads is no way to communicate. And besides . . ."

"But Dad . . ."

His father rolled on. It was impossible to get through to him. The lump came back into Russell's throat. The fuse was lit.

"Now, the next time this kid Eddie gives you trouble, I want you to . . ."

"Dad . . ."

". . . inform the teacher . . ."

The fuse was burning faster.

"Dad . . ."

". . . her duty to see that . . ."

The explosion was getting nearer.

"Dad?"

". . . students are protected . . ."

"Dad!"

". . . from situations like . . ."

KA-BOOM!

*"Dad, will you be quiet for once and listen to what I have to say?"* screamed Russell.

His father blinked and lapsed into a stunned silence. Russell's cheeks turned red. He couldn't believe what he had just done. He felt like getting out of the car and running.

But he couldn't. This might be the only time in his life that his father would be speechless.

"Dad, listen. The teachers can't help. The only time

2 6

Eddie and I are together is in the cafeteria and on the playground, when there's hundreds of kids around. Even if a teacher is watching, Eddie punches me anyway and gets in trouble for the fun of it. He doesn't care. I've been trying to tell you that. But you won't listen. You never listen. You're always too busy talking. *And it's driving me crazy!*"

His father stared straight ahead and drove without speaking.

Russell waited until he couldn't stand it any longer. "Well, say something!" he cried.

His father blinked. "I didn't know you felt that way," he said. "I thought I was helping you . . . offering guidance . . . showing you better ways to live. I always thought I listened to your problems. I've tried to be a good father, Russell. Goodness knows, it's hard enough these days . . ."

"Dad."

His father blushed. "I'm doing it again, aren't I?" he said softly.

"It's all right," said Russell. "I suppose it's a habit by now."

"But it's a habit I'm going to break," said Mr. Crannaker firmly. Then he bit his lips and they rode for a while in silence.

"Listen, Russell," he said at last. "About this Eddie thing. I really don't know what to say to help you now.

"Maybe that's why I said so much.

"But I'll think about it. And I want you to come to

talk to me if you have more problems with him. Next time I'll listen. Scout's honor."

Russell smiled. "Thanks, Dad."

His father smiled back. "I guess I haven't listened to much of anything you might have to say lately. Let's catch up some." He paused to think. "Oh—Halloween's this Saturday. Are you dressing up this year?"

Russell sighed. "I don't know. I *was* going to dress up, but some of the kids are saying that's baby stuff."

"Oh, I don't think so. Aren't any of them dressing up?"

"Well, Jack is working on an alien costume. It should be neat."

"That's good," said Mr. Crannaker. "Jack always did act a little like he came from another planet."

Russell chuckled. "And Sam is going to be a fat lady."

Mr. Crannaker made a face.

"And Jimmy Riblin says he's going to put mayonnaise in his mouth and be a pimple."

"*Yuk!*"

Russell laughed out loud. "Jimmy always was the weirdest kid in the class."

"But what about you, Russell? You're so interested in monsters, I would think you would want to dress up like one."

And that was when it struck him.

He didn't need a costume.

*He had his ring!*

Russell began to chuckle. He laughed out loud.

What an incredible idea! There had never, in the history of the world, been a costume like the one he was going to wear this Halloween.

Mr. Crannaker looked at Russell. "Are you all right?" he asked.

"Sure," gasped Russell. "I'm all right. Believe me, Dad, everything is just fine."

He chuckled to himself all the way home.

# FIVE

# Eddie's Revenge

"Now class, if a vampire has three quarts on deposit at the blood bank, and he takes out a pint and a half, how many cups are left?"

Russell smiled. For a fifth-grade teacher, Miss Snergal wasn't bad.

In fact, the whole week had been okay, considering how it had started. Oh, Henry "The Beast" Rafschnitz had been keeping a close eye on him. But he had been his usual quiet self, so that was no problem.

And he had actually gotten the feeling that Miss Snergal was pleased that he had stood up to Eddie.

As for Eddie himself, he seemed to be avoiding Russell. Maybe he had been put off by the tough talk outside the cafeteria doors. Whatever the reason, Russell enjoyed it while it lasted.

Best of all, Halloween was almost here. Of course, that meant he had to deal with his mother's usual reaction to anything involving lots of sweets. ("Eat all that sugar, Russell, and you'll have so many holes in your mouth you could pump air through it and play 'Hail, Columbia' on your teeth!") But he was used to that.

Besides, for him Halloween wasn't candy. It was mystery. Mystery, and a strange tingle, and dreams of ghosts and witches.

And—this year—a perfect opportunity to use his ring.

Friday, the day of the class party, arrived at last. In the morning Russell carefully packed a grocery sack with some old clothes he had snatched from the ragbag. Then he put his books on top of them so nobody would see his "costume." Finally he slipped the ring into his pocket and glanced over the instruction sheet to make sure he had the chants firmly in mind.

Soon he was on his bike, heading for school and feeling wonderful. This was going to be the greatest Halloween party of his life.

"Going someplace, Crannaker?"

Russell looked up, and his pleasant dreams came crashing down around him.

There was Eddie, standing in front of him on the sidewalk. His bike was drawn across the pavement, blocking Russell's path.

Russell tried to swallow the lump in his throat. He looked around for help. There was none in sight—no one to stop Eddie from turning him into a pulp.

Eddie grinned. "I owe you one, buster."

Russell fumbled for the ring. He pulled it from his pocket, started to put it on.

Whack! Eddie knocked the ring from his hand.

"Hey!" cried Russell, diving for it.

"Come here, twerp," yelled Eddie. He leapt after Russell. Just as Russell reached the ring, Eddie landed on his back with a crashing thump. Russell's fingers knocked against the ring. It rolled over the curb and into the gutter.

"Get off me, you bully!" screamed Russell.

Eddie laughed. "So you're not as tough as you thought, huh, Crannaker?"

He mashed Russell's face into the grass.

"Leave me alone!" cried Russell. But all that came out was "Leemealun!" Frustrated, he began to kick wildly. He felt one foot connect with Eddie's back.

"So you wanna get rough, huh?" screamed Eddie. He smashed Russell a good one, knocking the breath completely out of him. Then he climbed off.

"Remember that the next time you're thinking of calling *me* a bozo, Crannaker."

Russell pulled himself up from the grass. Eddie was gone, and the golden morning with him. A fierce anger burned in Russell's breast.

He crawled to the edge of the gutter. There was the ring, lying in a small puddle. Russell pounded his fists in the grass. He wanted to go after Eddie, drag him off that bike, pound his ugly face in.

But he wouldn't, because he was afraid.

He picked up the ring and put it in his pocket. Then he sat in the grass and sobbed. When the pain had gone down, he picked himself up and pedaled home to get ready for school again.

Russell's mother fussed over him as if the wounds had been made by bullets instead of fists.

"Why does this boy beat up on you anyway, Russell?" she asked as she was driving him to school.

Russell shrugged. "He hates me."

"Why does he hate you?"

"He hates everyone, I guess."

"That's too bad. Why don't you try to make friends with him?"

Russell looked at his mother in astonishment. She had to be kidding. "Make friends with Eddie? He'd kill me, Ma."

"I don't think so, Russell. The next time he wants to fight, just stick out your hand and say, 'Let's be friends.' You might be surprised at what happens."

"Yeah. Big surprise. He turns me into applesauce."

But Russell thought about his mother's words throughout the morning. One thing was certain. It would take as much guts to shake hands with Eddie as it would to punch him. Russell didn't think he could do it.

Anyway, he wasn't at all sure he *wanted* to make friends with someone who had just about killed him a few hours ago.

Russell's anger simmered within him through the

day. And it was a long day. The hours seemed to drag. All he could think of was the party, and using the ring once more.

At last it was time to put on the costumes. Miss Snergal sent those kids who had a lot of changing to do out of the room.

Jack and Jimmy went with Russell to the big bathroom down the hall. (Jimmy had decided against being a pimple. He was dressing up like broccoli instead. He said it was the most horrifying thing he could think of.)

While they were getting on their costumes, Russell went into one of the toilet stalls. He put on the old clothes he had brought. Then he took out the ring and slipped it onto his finger.

He looked at it for a moment, wondering who had made it. The monster on the top seemed to be looking back at him. Suddenly he was more eager than ever to be a monster himself. His thoughts went back to that morning. He could feel his anger at Eddie welling up again, and with it an aching urge for revenge.

He made his decision.

Taking firm hold of the ring, Russell chanted the verse from the instruction sheet. At the same time he turned the ring once . . . and then again.

# Double Whammy

Russell felt like he had been kicked by a mule and then dropped into a vat of ice water. Everything that had happened before was happening again, but faster. He grew hot and cold by turns. There was a terrible itching under his skin. He could feel horns and hair bursting through.

He waited. He couldn't leave the stall before the change was done. It wouldn't do to have Jack and Jimmy see his horns growing before their very eyes!

"Hey, Russell!" yelled Jack. "Hurry up! We're ready to go!"

"I'm coming," he growled. "Hold your horses."

He touched his horns. They were complete. His hands, covered with thick black fur, had sharp claws curling down from the fingertips. As he watched they stopped growing.

He opened the door and stepped out.

"Good grief, Russell!" cried Jack. "That's incredible!"

"Where did you get it?" yelled Jimmy.

Russell could hear the jealousy in their voices. His "costume" was the kind of thing every kid dreamed of.

He shrugged. "I made it from stuff we had around the house."

He sounded like a gorilla with a sore throat.

Jack and Jimmy gaped. "How did you do *that*?" Jack cried.

Russell smiled. "It's a secret."

He stepped up to the mirror to examine himself and almost screamed.

He was ten times more horrible than he had been after the first change. His horns were longer and a brilliant fire-red. Hair sprang out all around his head, almost like a lion's mane. His nose was flat and shiny. And large fangs gleamed in his mouth—sharp things, deadly looking, made for ripping and tearing.

He remembered the lines on the instruction sheet:

Twist it once, you're horned and haired;
Twist it twice and fangs are bared. . . .

But it was his eyes that did the trick. They seemed to be twice their normal size and set more deeply into his head. They had dark, evil-looking rings around them and thick, bloodshot lines running in from the corners. Most incredible of all, the irises had turned red!

"Come on, Russell!" urged Jack. "I can't wait for Miss Snergal to see this!"

He threw his arm around Russell's shoulder. Jimmy did the same thing. This monster was theirs.

Russell was delighted. But as they were walking toward their classroom something happened that should have made him worry. Without warning, without knowing why, he suddenly lifted his head and let out a long, mournful howl that echoed down the corridor.

Doors flew open as teachers looked for the source of the sound. Their faces were priceless. Jack almost fell over laughing, and Jimmy had to hold on to Russell's arm to support himself.

Outside their own room they paused to prepare a grand entry. Jack swung the door open. Jimmy stepped in and bowed. "Ladies and gentlemen!" he cried. "Allow me to present to you the *real* Beast of Boardman Road!"

Then Russell was supposed to step into the room and stand there so everyone could ooh and ah over his fantastic costume.

But something happened. He didn't step through the door. He leaped through, growling ferociously. A second leap and he was standing on Missy Freebaker's desk, snarling fiercely. He turned warily about, baring his fangs, ready to attack the first thing that moved.

His effect on the class was electric. The girls screamed. The boys squeaked. Everyone seemed poised to run.

Miss Snergal clapped her hands and broke the spell. "Come, come," she said. "Enough of this. Russell, that is certainly the most magnificent costume I have ever seen. But it does not justify this outrageous behavior."

Russell shook his head. He looked around and saw the horrified faces of his classmates.

"I'm sorry, Miss Snergal," he growled. "I got carried away."

She jumped at the sound of his voice.

"I should say so," she said, looking at him curiously.

Suddenly the class came to life. They surged forward to examine Russell.

"Take off the mask, Russ! I want to see how it fastens on."

"How'd you do the ears?"

"Where did you get those teeth?"

"Tell me how you put on the fur!"

"Now, class," said Miss Snergal, "perhaps Russell has some professional secrets that he would rather not divulge." She gave Russell a wink.

He smiled back, showing her a mouthful of fangs. She looked startled but went on addressing the class.

"Now let's clear our desks. As soon as the parade's over we'll have our party."

A cheer went up. Before long they were heading for the gym and the school-wide costume parade. Things went well until Russell spotted Mr. Rafschnitz. Then the hair on the back of his neck stood up and his lip began to curl. A snarl was welling up in his throat. There was nothing he could do to stop it. Stretching out his claws, he began to snap at Mr. Rafschnitz.

The principal looked horrified—and it was not an act.

It was Jack who saved the day. Thinking that Russell was playing, he decided to get in on the fun. "Down, boy!" he shouted. "Down! Supper is waiting in the dungeon. Down. Down, beast!"

Russell gave Mr. Rafschnitz a snarl for good measure and followed Jack around the gymnasium.

"I've got to hand it to you, Russell," said Jack. "You've got more guts than I have. No one ever dared to growl at the Beast like that. Not even Tough Eddie."

When Russell bounded back into the classroom, Mrs. Elmore, the room mother, took one look at him and almost dropped the tray of cookies she was carrying.

The party started. The kids swarmed into the goodies like starving hamsters let loose in a vegetable bin. But Russell wasn't interested. He did try a candy pumpkin, but it stuck in his fangs, and after that he just sat there growling and snorting.

It was the games that really started the trouble, though. The first hint of disaster came when they played Bite the Apple. Mrs. Elmore had threaded apples on strings and hung them from the ceiling. The kids were supposed to stand face to face and try to catch them with their teeth.

Russell was teamed up with Frieda Mollis. When the apple slipped away from him, he got angry and started snapping at it. Then he started snapping at Frieda. She screamed. Miss Snergal ran over crying, "Really, Russell, you must control yourself!"

"Sorry," he growled.

But he wasn't. He had enjoyed it. He wanted to growl and snap some more.

He wanted to run around and howl.

He wanted to scare the living daylights out of people!

And he got his chance. The next game was called Ugly Face. The class split into two lines facing each other. Then everyone had to make the ugliest face they could. Whoever laughed was out.

Russell thought this was a good idea. When the game started, he looked at Georgie Smud and just curled up his lips. But Georgie didn't laugh. He looked scared. That was fine with Russell. He curled his lips even more and snarled. Georgie yelled. Russell began to jump up and down. He ran along the line, snarling and growling, trying to scare the other team all at once.

"Russell!"

Miss Snergal again.

He held in his growl and bowed his head.

"Sorry."

"Just watch it." She turned to face the rest of the class. "I think it's time for the story," she said.

They had been looking forward to this. It was the best day of the year for stories, and Miss Snergal had already explained her plans to them.

First she turned off the lights. Then she lit the jack-o'-lantern. Wrapping a cape about her shoulders, she hobbled to a corner and sat down. She crooked a finger and said in a creaky voice, "Come, children. Come to the Halloween corner to hear a tale of terror."

She was a good actress, and the class was in the right mood to believe that she really was a wicked witch.

"Once upon a time there was a witch who lived in a cottage in the forest. Late at night, when the moon was high, she would dance around her crackling fire and stir her bubbling caldron."

The story began to do something to Russell. He felt a howl rising up inside him.

"One day a handsome prince came riding up to the cottage. He was dressed all in white and carried a sword at his side."

Russell felt his lip begin to curl as he took an instant dislike to the handsome prince.

When the witch gave the prince a magic sword and sent him on a quest for a monster, Russell began to squirm.

When Miss Snergal reached the part where the moon was full and the prince was riding into a great forest to find the monster and kill it, Russell felt like he was going to jump out of his skin.

And when the prince raised his sword and was about to run the monster through, Russell finally broke. The howls and snarls that had been building up inside of him would wait no longer. Tipping back his head, he poured out a long, mournful wail that caused even Miss Snergal's blood to run cold in her veins.

Kill the monster indeed!

# SEVEN

# Russell Goes Berserk

Russell leapt to his feet. The beast in his blood was going wild. Some of the kids screamed. Others began to edge away from him.

"Russell, stop that this instant!" snapped Miss Snergal. The story-telling witch was gone; the teacher was back.

Russell snarled at her. Inside him, someplace, a tiny voice was saying, "This is crazy. Crazy! Stop it. Stop it now!"

But the monster part of him wouldn't listen to the voice. His snarl became a growl. Suddenly he realized what he wanted to do.

*Get Eddie!*

With a roar he charged across the hall to Mrs. Brown's room. There was a squeal of terror from the

kids. Russell saw Eddie's eyes pop open in surprise. Everyone ran to the corner farthest from the door. Russell jumped onto a desk, growling and snapping.

"Young man, you get down from there this instant!" cried Mrs. Brown. When he didn't move, she grabbed her broom and whacked him.

Russell yelped with rage and jumped off the desk. He headed for the corner where the children had huddled.

At that moment Miss Snergal staggered into the room.

"Russell!" she cried.

He glanced over his shoulder. But it was too late. He couldn't stop now. Raising his claws, he headed for Eddie.

"Oh no you don't!" yelled Mrs. Brown. She hit him on the head with her broom.

Russell spun about in a blind rage. Mrs. Brown whacked him again.

Half the children were laughing, the other half were crying. Russell was roaring with outrage. "Get out of here, whoever you are," snapped Mrs. Brown. "And don't come back!"

The Russell-monster hesitated, torn between getting at Eddie and getting away from Mrs. Brown. He turned back toward Eddie and snarled again. Mrs. Brown swatted him across the backside.

That was enough for Russell. He ran for the door. Mrs. Brown charged after him crying, "Out of my room, you ruffian!"

Russell vaulted a desk, shot through the door, and ran smack dab into a class walking down the hallway. He dashed through the middle of them, growling and snarling.

Kids were screaming and shouting. They split to let him pass. He sped down the hall, rounded the corner—and ran straight into another class!

He turned and ran back the way he had come. But the first class had decided to chase him. It was too late to stop; he plunged into their midst. Shrieking and giggling, they pulled at his fur. The monster side of him went wild. A huge roar broke from his lungs. The children shrank back, and he escaped.

But at once they were after him again—joined now by the class he had met turning the corner!

The rumpus attracted the children still in their rooms. Doors flew open. Heedless of their teachers' cries, the kids poured into the hallway to join the merry chase.

Merry for everyone but Russell. Yelping in fright, he was skidding around the corners and down the halls as fast as his powerful legs would carry him. But the floors were freshly waxed. He slipped and slid and couldn't get a lead on his pursuers.

He dodged into the cafeteria. The mob followed. Russell took to the tabletops. In several great leaps he made it from one side of the lunchroom to the other. The pursuing mass of children had to split and flow along the narrow spaces between the tables.

He was ahead of them!

And just ahead of him there was another door, and past that the doors to the outside, and freedom.

But suddenly there he was, standing in the doorway—the original Beast of Boardman Road, Mr. Henry Rafschnitz himself!

For a moment Russell panicked. Then the monster side took over. Standing on the edge of a table, he gave a deep-throated growl, flexed his legs, and leaped straight at the principal. Mr. Rafschnitz held his ground for an instant. Then, as he saw that the monster really intended to land on him, he turned pale and ducked. Russell shot past him into the hall and then out through the big glass doors.

He was free!

Miss Snergal had made it to the head of the chase. She ran after him just before Mr. Rafschnitz barred the doors.

"Russell," she cried. "Come back! I want to talk to you!"

But the sunlight was bringing Russell to his senses. He was terrified.

There was a little wood behind the school. He headed for it. Scrambling up an old oak, he hid behind the scarlet leaves.

The ring was glowing. Russell grabbed at it with his claws.

It wouldn't turn!

He tried again. But his monster paws were larger than his hands. The ring was too tight!

He strained mightily. At last it began to move.

Repeating the verse, he turned the ring twice.

Seconds later the beast was gone.

In its place sat Russell.

Quiet Russell, who had frightened three classes, snarled at two teachers, and terrified one principal.

Timid Russell, who had started the first riot in the history of Boardman Road Elementary School.

Quiet, timid Russell, who was in more trouble than he had ever dreamed of in his entire life.

# EIGHT

# The Beast Within

The next morning dawned clear and bright.

Halloween!

Russell bounded out of bed with unusual energy, impatient for the night when the day had hardly begun.

He sailed down the stairs and into the kitchen. Breakfast was ready. He took his place at the table.

"I want to talk to you, Russell."

He froze, a spoonful of organic oatmeal halfway to his mouth. His mother was looking at him intently.

"About yesterday."

He put down the spoon.

"Russell, why were you up in that tree when I came to get you?"

"I told you. The kids chased me out of school."

"Yes. Mr. Rafschnitz told me the same thing when he called. But he also said that you had caused a riot. I said that was impossible."

Russell started to relax.

"Then I talked to Jack's mother this morning. She said Jack told her you acted like a real maniac. Why did he say that, Russell?"

Russell sighed. There was no sense in hiding it now. "Because it's true."

"But it can't be! I know you better than that. You would never misbehave so badly."

Russell was a little irked. What did she think he was, a plastic angel? He was perfectly capable of misbehaving. He thrust out his chin, about to say so. Then he looked at his mother. Her eyes were pleading with him to say he hadn't done it. More to the point, they were telling him she wouldn't believe even if he had.

He sighed. "You're right, Ma. It isn't true. I don't know why Jack said that. I think he's mad at me. All the kids are out to get me. They all hate me."

He was so convincing he began to feel sorry for himself.

"There, there, Russell," said his mother, putting her arm around his shoulder and patting him. "I'll talk to Miss Snergal. Mother will make it better."

Russell pushed away from her smothering embrace. "I don't want you to make it better!" he cried. "Why won't you ever let me make something better myself?"

It was hard to tell which of them was more shocked.

His mother looked at him with hurt eyes. Her lip began to tremble. Russell pushed away from the table and ran from the house.

He plopped down in a little park about two blocks from home. Sitting beneath a large oak tree, he clenched his fists and began to pound the piles of dead leaves that surrounded him.

Why did she treat him like such a baby? How could he grow up if he never got the chance?

He picked up an acorn and threw it.

"Ouch!"

Russell looked up. There was Eddie, standing astride his bicycle, not ten feet away. He had a strange look on his face—a combination of anger, amusement, and (could it be?) fear. He paused, then hopped off the bike and sauntered over to where Russell sat.

"Well, Crannaker, that was some outfit you had on in school yesterday. Made you feel pretty brave, didn't it?"

"Oh, go play in the road, toad," said Russell.

The look on Eddie's face tightened, and Russell saw him begin to ball his hands into fists. "What did you say, Crannaker?"

"You heard me, peabrain. Go lick your finger and stick it in a socket."

Russell nearly laughed out loud at the look on Eddie's face. It occurred to him that he was doing something very dangerous. He didn't care.

Eddie stepped closer.

Russell stood up. For the first time he could remember, he made a fist with the intention of using it on someone. He had the feeling that he was going to get pounded again. But this time he was going to pound back.

Suddenly he wasn't sure he wanted to. Fighting was stupid.

He tightened his fists anyway and brought them up against his sides. He could feel a snarl creeping up his throat. This was exciting! Suddenly he wanted to howl, had an urge to leap on Eddie with claws and fangs going all at once.

That scared him.

He looked at his hands, half expecting them to be sprouting fur.

He took a deep breath, lowered his fists, and said, "Look, Eddie, I don't want to fight. . . ."

"Of course you don't," sneered Eddie. "You're a chicken! Bawk ba bawk ba bawk." He pushed Russell's shoulder.

It wasn't a hard push. But it made something inside Russell snap.

"You idiot!" he cried.

Then he jumped.

Eddie's eyes went wide. He cried out in fear.

Russell had become a whirlwind of thrashing arms and flailing legs. Eddie toppled beneath his onslaught. Holding his enemy down, Russell opened his mouth to take a bite out of Eddie's shoulder.

That's when the warning bell went off in his head.

"What am I doing?" he cried in horror.

Terrified now, not of Eddie but of himself, he leaped to his feet and raced off. He ran for blocks, afraid that if he stopped, something awful would happen.

At last his body forced him to halt. Panting, gasping, he leaned against a building and let the question rage through his brain.

What was this ring doing to him?

There was only one place to go for an answer.

Elives' magic shop.

# NINE

# The Third Twist
# of the Ring

Russell sat in his room, staring at the ring.

It scared him.

He loved it—loved the monstrous carving, the magic that it contained.

But he was frightened by what was happening to him.

He was frightened, too, because of what he had found when he went back to the magic shop.

What he had found was nothing. No matter how hard he'd tried, and he had spent a good two hours at it, he had been unable to retrace the steps that had taken him to S. H. Elives' mysterious little store.

Russell looked at the ring again. So far it had gotten him into more trouble than he was willing to think about.

But—it had also been a lot of fun.

Should he use it tonight, or not?

Common sense was saying no.

But another side of him, a wilder side, was saying, "It's *Halloween*! What better time to be a monster?"

He *had* been looking forward to this night all week.

He looked at the instruction sheet lying on his desk.

Twist it once, you're horned and haired;
Twist it twice and fangs are bared;
Twist it thrice? No one has dared!

Well, he had felt very daring lately.

He smiled. One good thing—he didn't have to make up his mind right away. With the ring he could put on his "costume" anytime he wanted to.

He put the directions in an envelope and tucked them away in his dresser for safekeeping. Then he went downstairs. His mother was in the den, reading.

"I'm going to the bonfire now," he said.

"All right, Russell. Have a good time."

He looked at her, feeling guilty about his outburst that morning. Suddenly he gave her a quick kiss on the cheek. Then he scooted out the door.

Every year the town council held a bonfire at the high school to keep the kids out of mischief on Halloween. They organized games, served cider and donuts, and gave prizes for the best costumes. It was a good time, and Russell always looked forward to it.

This year they had a perfect night for it. There was a tang in the air, a full moon, and a sprinkling of stars and clouds across an ebony sky.

The crowd was in a happy mood. Russell nabbed a cup of cider, crammed half a donut in his mouth, and wandered off to see how the bobbing for apples was going. Suddenly he spotted Eddie out of the corner of his eye. He was in the grip of a large, mean-looking teenager. There was a frightened expression on his face.

Watching as the older boy steered Eddie through the crowd, Russell decided to follow. He trailed them around the corner of the school, pressing himself to the building so that he wouldn't be seen. It was dark back there.

Two other teenagers stepped out from the shadows. Russell edged closer to the four figures, listening intently.

"Aw, come on, you guys," said Eddie. "I didn't do anything that bad."

Russell recognized the nervous edge in Eddie's voice. He had heard it often enough in his own.

"Of course you didn't," sneered one of the boys. "We just want to teach you a lesson now, before you do anything worse."

Another reached into Eddie's shirt pocket. "Here's his soap. He was gonna soap more windows."

"Maybe we should soap him," said the third boy. "How about that, punk? Wanna take a bath in the river?"

"Yeah. And then you can play Find Your Clothes," said the first with a laugh.

Russell began to get edgy. He fingered his ring.

Eddie made a break for it. One of the boys grabbed him. "Help!" cried Eddie.

"Shut up, punk!" snapped the boy. He slapped Eddie sharply.

That did it. Russell began to twist the ring, repeating the chant as he did so. Once, twice, and, in the heat of his anger, a third time the ring turned on his finger.

There was a small explosion in his head, and he knew at once, with a deep conviction, that this change was going to be very different.

The boys were dragging Eddie off. Russell started to follow. Then he staggered and fell back into the shadow of a doorway. The change was too fast, too strong. He couldn't move.

All the familiar things were happening—the horns, the fangs, the hair on hands and feet. But there was something else going on, too, something strange and new. He felt like someone had reached down inside of him, grabbed his toes, and was trying to turn him inside out.

He was hot and cold by alternate flashes.

A foul odor was emanating from his skin.

And suddenly he was scared, scared to the bottom of his soul.

"No one has dared," the instructions had said.

Had he gone too far?

He became aware of a stabbing pain in his back. It

increased in intensity until he fell to the ground, writhing in agony. There was a sudden rush of even more intense pain, sharp and flamelike ... a tearing sound ... a feeling that he was being ripped apart ... and then the impossible happened.

Up from his shoulders sprang two huge, batlike wings.

But there was no time to even think about that. The heat from his body had become unbearable. Lifting himself to his hands and knees, he saw the hair on the backs of his hands begin to smoke.

The heat grew more intense. He realized with sudden horror that his clothes were smoking, too. Desperate, he tore at them. Too late. They had reached the flash point. In one horrible moment he was wrapped in flames from head to toe.

# TEN

# Russell to
# the Rescue

Russell cried out in terror. But as quickly as they had begun, the flames died away.

Slowly he rose to his feet. He stood straight, then stretched toward the beckoning moon.

And if he had been a monster before, Russell Crannaker was a king among monsters now.

He was magnificent. His entire body was covered with overlapping red scales that gleamed like burnished metal. His wings stretched tall behind him, their peaks and points looming against the night. And in his eyes there burned a fire that could freeze a man with fear.

He extended his wings, flapped twice, and floated into the air.

For an instant, even though it was his own power that carried him, he panicked. He felt as though he had been plucked from the earth, was being carried away.

The feeling of captivity disappeared as he realized that he was his own master.

Working the wings, he rose higher into the night, pulling his body into the deep black heavens. He watched the ground shrink away as he drew level with the treetops, then continued to rise, on and up, toward the mysterious moon.

How high could he go?

He decided to find out. But when he had soared up to about three hundred feet, he looked down. Suddenly he felt like he had just taken a dive on the biggest roller coaster in the world. His stomach was begging for mercy.

He dropped back to about a hundred feet. That was better. He began to glide lazily over the town.

He found it deeply satisfying to be up there under his own power. The silence, no sound save the wind on his wings, made it seem almost as though he had entered another world, separate from the one that drifted below him, so very far away.

Passing over the school, he saw the bonfire and three or four hundred costumed children, looking like beetles as they milled about, guzzling cider and cramming donuts.

He swooped down toward them. There was a flurry of exclamations, pointing, screaming—and then he was gone, leaving them wondering, but happy. He had made their Halloween.

He soared up again, past the school. Suddenly he saw four figures, three large ones and a smaller one, struggling wildly.

Eddie!

Russell had forgotten all about him in the heat of the transformation. He was in trouble. And despite the past, three against one stuck in Russell's throat.

The monster side of Russell snapped into action.

First came the roar. It was ear-splitting. Thundering through the night, it spun the teenagers around. Their eyes bulged with horror. They looked as if they were seeing the end of the world.

And as far as they were concerned, they were. For Russell looked like nothing so much as death on wings, descending now to claim them.

"Move!" screamed one. They dropped Eddie and headed down the street as fast as their legs would carry them.

But Russell's hunting blood was roused. He shot after them like an arrow from a bow.

The great wings working furiously, he sped along a mere five feet above the pavement. His blood roared through his veins, pounding with the joy of the chase. He closed on the boy in the rear. Catching him under the arms with his claws, Russell changed direction and headed straight up.

"Helllp!" screamed his captive. "Let me down! Let me down!"

He began to kick wildly.

"Be careful," growled Russell, "or I might drop you."

They were about a hundred feet in the air.

The boy stopped kicking.

Russell continued to rise, thrilled with the strength in his usually puny arms, until he was above the tallest building in the town. The land had become like a map beneath them, the houses small squares, the streets little lines.

The moon sparkled on the river at the west edge of the town. Russell swooped toward the black and silver water. "How would *you* like a bath?" he asked, remembering how the boys had threatened Eddie.

Eddie! As long as he was at it, maybe he ought to give *him* a good scare. Not hurt him, as these jokers had intended. Just—educate him a little.

Suddenly he lost interest in the rowdy dangling from his talons. "Remember this the next time you decide to pick on someone," he growled. Swooping even lower, he dropped the boy in the mud at the river's edge. He rose again, banked in a sharp curve, and zoomed back toward Eddie.

Eddie was crouched in the back entrance of the high school, a glazed expression on his face. Russell landed about fifteen feet in front of him. Eddie jumped up, pressing himself against the locked door.

"Get away from me," he cried. "Get away, you monster. Don't come near me!"

"Be quiet," snarled Russell. His voice was ferocious.

"Right," said Eddie. "Anything you say."

"Now look," said Russell. "You've been picking on a friend of mine."

Eddie looked blank.

"Russell Crannaker. I want you to leave him alone."

The look on Eddie's face changed to pure astonishment. Russell bared his fangs. "Right," said Eddie quickly. "I leave him alone, and you leave me alone. Right?"

"You've got it," said Russell. "But don't forget—or you'll be very, very sorry."

Roaring with laughter, he soared into the air.

About fifty feet away he touched down beside a tree, still chuckling. That was the most satisfying thing he had ever done. Now to change back—and test Eddie's resolution to leave him alone.

He grasped the ring. It was hard to turn. But his claws were strong. He twisted it on his finger and said the familiar words.

Nothing happened.

ELEVEN

# Partners

Russell couldn't believe it.

He must have done something wrong.

He tried again.

Nothing.

Absolutely nothing.

He tried again . . . and again . . . and again.

It was no use. The ring wasn't working!

Now what?

The directions. He had to get the directions!

Stretching his wings, Russell soared into the air and headed for home.

Good. The backyard was empty. Folding his wings, he dropped straight down. He extended them just in time to break the fall. Then he floated to his bedroom and stuck his head through the window.

To his horror, that was all he could stick through. No matter how he folded his wings behind him, they were too big to pass the frame.

He was trapped outside!

*Now* what?

He flew away from the house, thinking desperately.

Suddenly he saw Eddie below him. He was walking slowly, leaning on the buildings for support. Perfect! Russell dropped down in front of him.

"What do you want now?" screamed Eddie. "I told you I'd leave Russell alone."

"I have to talk to you," said Russell, trying to keep his voice from booming too much. "Step in here." He motioned to a nearby alley where they could be out of sight.

Eddie hesitated.

Russell pulled back his lips in a fang-baring frown.

Eddie went into the alley.

"Now look," Russell said once they were out of sight. "I saved you from those teenagers, right?"

"Yes. . . ."

"So you know I'm not going to hurt you, right?"

"I guess so."

"Good. I didn't do that for Russell."

He paused.

"I *am* Russell."

Eddie looked blank.

"This is me, Eddie. Russell. Russell Crannaker."

Eddie stared at him incredulously. "What do you mean, you're Russell? That's impossible."

"Do you remember yesterday in school?" asked Russell.

"You mean when Russell wore that crazy costume and ... and ..." A look of astonishment grew in Eddie's eyes. "*You mean that wasn't a costume?*"

Russell shook his head from side to side.

Eddie turned even paler. His eyes got wide. His lips worked, but the only sound that came out was "Buh ... buh ... buh ..."

He looked like a goldfish.

Russell smiled. He had a feeling Eddie had just decided he'd been taking his life in his hands every time he had bothered poor, puny Russell Crannaker.

Finally Eddie found his voice. "Uh ... how come you let me get away with all that stuff?"

He squeaked. It was pathetic.

Inspiration struck. "Oh, punks like you don't bother me."

Russell was inwardly delighted. That offhand dismissal should finish convincing Eddie that Russell could have destroyed him at any time. It ought to keep him safe for the rest of his life.

*If* he ever got to *be* Russell again!

He became aware that Eddie was talking. ". . . so thanks for saving me from those kids."

"It was nothing," said Russell. "I just didn't like their style." He tried to sound casual. "But as long as you appreciated it, there *is* something you could do to help me in return."

"Sure," said Eddie quickly. "Anything."

"There's something I need in my room. It's not easy for me to get it until I change back. So I want you to get it for me."

"You got it," said Eddie. "Just tell me how to get in."

"I'll fly you there."

Eddie blanched.

"What's the matter?" asked Russell dryly. "You're not afraid, are you?"

"No! It's just that . . . no, I'm not afraid. Let's go."

"Okay," said Russell. He stepped from the shadows. When Eddie saw him up close, saw how truly hideous he had become, he shrank back again. Russell waited a moment for him to recover, then plucked him up and flew.

When they reached the house, Russell coasted to the window and put Eddie on the sill. "Now listen," he hissed. "In the middle drawer of that dresser there's a small white envelope. Get it for me."

The fierce insistence in his voice was all the motivation Eddie needed. He scooted to the dresser and pulled the drawer open. Socks flew in all directions.

"I don't see it," he whispered.

"Then look in the next one down!"

"All right." He pulled open the drawer and began to paw through it.

"Hurry!" snapped Russell.

Suddenly they heard the sound of footsteps in the hall. Eddie's head whipped around. "Someone's coming!"

"Keep looking!"

Eddie was wild with fear. "But if I get caught here I'll be arrested!"

"LOOK!" roared Russell.

Sweat beaded out on Eddie's brow. He scrabbled frantically in the bottom drawer.

The doorknob turned.

"I've got it!"

"Jump!"

Mr. Crannaker burst into the room just in time to see Eddie vanish over the sill.

# Return to the Magic Shop

For a sickening instant Russell was not certain he could catch Eddie. But his powerful arms did the job almost instinctively. Snatching him up in mid-fall, Russell soared into the sky, Eddie dangling and gasping below him.

"Good grief!" panted Eddie.

"Good job," said Russell. "I'll remember it."

Mr. Crannaker stuck his head out the window, craning his neck as he scanned the ground to catch sight of whoever had just been in the room.

It never did occur to him to look up.

"Where to?" asked Russell.

"Home will be fine," said Eddie weakly.

Russell set Eddie down beside a tree about a hundred feet from his home. They parted friends, or as near to that state as they were ever likely to get. Russell extended a claw, and Eddie gave him the envelope. Then they shook, hand and claw, Eddie repeating his vow that he would never bother Russell again.

Russell was pleased. But in truth, Eddie was the least of his worries now. Leaving him as quickly as possible, Russell flew off to find a place where he could be alone.

Finally he landed on the flat, empty roof of Boardman Road Elementary.

He stared at the envelope, almost afraid to open it. He was more and more troubled by the memory of that line—"No one has dared."

Was that a challenge, as he had believed—or a warning?

His heart turned cold at the thought. With trembling claws he extracted the crumpled paper. And then the moonlight, shining over his shoulder, struck another line that he had ignored, one vitally important instruction that he hadn't even considered.

"Use with caution, *and never on the night of a full moon.*"

He turned to the sky.

There it was—full and bright. Fuller, it now seemed, than he had ever seen it before.

*Never on the night of a full moon.*

He sighed heavily. With a dead thump of certainty he knew that he had made the ghastliest mistake of his life—three twists of a magic ring on the night of a great full moon.

He was ruined. There was no way out—no way to become plain old Russell Crannaker again.

Now that he thought about it, being plain old Russell Crannaker wasn't all that bad. He had a good home and loving parents. He had some friends. He did well in school. He had a teacher he enjoyed.

And it was gone, all gone, because he had been fool enough to use the ring—and use it to excess—on the night of a full moon.

Fool moon, they should call it.

He had been a fool to go into Elives' shop to begin with.

Elives! This was his fault. He had sold him the thing.

But maybe Elives knew a way out!

Russell took wing, hoping that he could spot the shop from above.

He soared over the town, searching desperately. There was the alley where he had played at being Frankenstein, a lifetime ago. There was the place where Eddie had slipped on the garbage. There was the street of little shops. And there ... there it was!

He landed in front of the magic shop, filled with a sense of relief. He glanced stealthily up and down the street. It was deserted.

He wondered what time it was. His parents would be out of their minds with worry. But what could he do? Walk in and say, "Hi! It's me—Russell. I made a little mistake with this magic ring I've been messing around with, and I'm going to be a monster from now on. You don't mind, do you?"

A sob tried to force its way through his monsterish throat as he realized, for good and all, that if he could not reverse this change he would never see his home and his parents again.

He pounded on the door. A light went on in the back of the shop. He looked around, afraid the noise would rouse someone else too.

The street was still empty.

"Let me in!" he cried, pounding with both fists. "Let me in!"

"I'm coming," called a voice from the back of the shop. "I'm coming. Pipe down."

Russell peered through the window. He could see the old man who had sold him the ring, shuffling toward the door. He had on a ratty-looking black bathrobe covered with moons and stars, and worn carpet slippers that kept sliding off his heels.

The door snapped open. "What are you trying to do? Raise the dead? There's enough of them up and around already tonight!"

The old man's eyes focused on Russell. He grabbed Russell's arm and pulled him into the shop, slamming the door behind him.

"So it's you," he said. There was a note of smugness in his voice. "I've been expecting you."

"What?"

"Oh, come, come," said the old man. "You hardly struck me as being the careful type when I sold you that ring. Hardly the type to pay attention to . . . vital instructions?"

Russell looked at the floor in shame.

"Well, what have you come for?" asked Elives.

Russell looked up in astonishment. "I want you to help me."

Elives threw up his hands in disgust. "I've helped you plenty," he said. "I sold you the ring, didn't I? What more do you want?"

"I want to change back!"

"Well, that's hardly my concern," he said. "I included very specific directions with that ring. Never use it on the night of a full moon. You can read, can't you?"

"Yes, of course, but—"

"But but but! Directions are directions. You follow them or you don't. What you choose to do with a thing once I sell it to you is none of my concern. If you can't be responsible for your actions, you can hardly expect *me* to take responsibility for them."

"But—"

"And furthermore, it is highly inconsiderate to come to my shop at this hour and rouse me out of a sound sleep. I work hard all day, and I don't need some moron who can't follow directions coming around in the middle of the night to disturb my rest."

Russell knew that if his monster self could cry, he

would be crying by now. But he wouldn't be ashamed of it this time. He had been wrong, really wrong.

He said the only thing he could think of.

"I'm sorry."

"Well, in that case," said Mr. Elives, "sit down for a minute. We'll talk." He motioned to a chair. Russell cleared away a top hat and a string of silk scarves and sat down, his wings spread on either side of the chair.

"You cast a nice shadow," said Elives approvingly.

Russell looked around at the peaked and pointed shadow made by his wings. "I'd just as soon get rid of it," he said softly.

"I'm well aware of that. Now, tell me. How many times have you used the ring?"

"Three."

"One twist, then two, and finally three?"

Russell nodded.

Elives scratched his chin. "Most people are bright enough to stop at two."

Russell blushed, but it was hidden by his flame-red cheeks.

"And on the night of a full moon." The old man sighed. "Well," he said at last, "you'll have to stay in that shape for a while yet."

Russell looked up with sudden hope.

"A while?"

Elives nodded. "With a ring like that, there's no way the antidote can take effect on the night of a full moon. She has powers of her own, you know. But things may be different tomorrow. We'll just have to wait and see." He shrugged. "If you'd like to spend the rest of the night here, you can sleep in that chair. I'm going to bed."

"Thank you," said Russell.

There was one thing still bothering him. "What will I tell my parents?"

"Tell them anything you want!" snapped Elives. "They're your problem. I can't solve all your troubles for you!" He paused. "And don't come running back to me if there are any aftereffects, either."

Russell looked up, about to ask what he meant. But the old man had turned and was heading toward the back of the shop. Russell sighed and leaned back in the chair.

He would deal with all that when he came to it.

Right now he only wanted to sleep.

# THIRTEEN

# Home Run

Russell woke with a start.

A cold gray light was leaking through the window. It was morning.

He looked down at his body. His body! He had it back. He was himself again!

He let out a whoop of joy.

"Shut up!" yelled a voice from the back of the shop.

Russell held in his excitement. But it wasn't easy. He wanted to sing—shout—dance. He was Russell Crannaker, fifth-grade boy, and Russell-the-monster was gone, gone, gone.

Then he realized he had a new problem.

He was stark naked!

His clothes had been burned off during his transformation the night before.

*Now* what was he going to do?

He sat for a moment, pondering the question. Finally, gathering his courage, he went to the back of the shop.

"Mr. Elives," he called quietly through the curtain.

"Go away!"

"Mr. Elives, I need your help."

"Go away. I've helped you enough!"

"But I don't have any clothes."

"That's not my fault."

"But how can I get home?"

"Walk!"

"I can't do that!"

"Young man, if you do not leave my shop soon, I will show you a blast of magic that will make that silly ring seem like a toy. Now go!"

Russell stepped away from the curtains.

He was naked! How could he go home?

On the other hand, how could he stay here?

He thought it over. Considering how much trouble he was in already, being naked when he got home wasn't going to make that much difference.

But when he reached the door, he couldn't force himself to open it. The idea that had almost made sense thirty seconds ago now seemed insane.

He tried to convince himself.

It was Sunday morning. It was only about six o'clock, and the light was still dim. Hardly anyone would be up at this hour.

Besides, the bare fact was, there was nothing else he *could* do. He *had* to make a run for it.

At last his hand obeyed his orders. He reached out, opened the door, and slipped through.

Immediately he felt that everyone in the town was looking at him. Even the buildings seemed to have eyes.

There was dead silence.

He began to run.

As he reached the corner he noticed that the ring was gone. It must have slipped off when his hand had returned to normal. He hesitated for a moment, uncertain. Did he want it back, or not?

He turned back toward the shop.

No. Gone was gone. It had caused him enough trouble already.

Besides, he didn't need it anymore.

So . . . good-bye, ring, and good-bye, Mr. Elives. He waved a hand in farewell and resumed the homeward run.

Once the first fright had passed, he actually began to enjoy it. The chill in the air—and the sheer craziness of racing across town in his birthday suit—made him wildly alert. He felt open to the world, delighted by every sight and sound his greedy senses could absorb.

By taking to the backyards, he managed to remain unseen until he reached the development where he lived. Then, scooting behind a gray house, he saw a tired-looking woman standing at a window, holding a cup of coffee and gazing out with her eyelids at half-mast.

When she saw Russell, it looked like someone had plugged in her curlers. Her eyelids shot up, her jaw dropped down, and coffee flew in all directions.

She strained to see who it was. But he was gone, trying not to let his laughter slow him down.

Five minutes later he was home. But he couldn't figure out the best way into the house. When you were a beast it was easy. You just scrambled up the side of the house and through a window.

There was no way to do that now.

In fact, the only way in was through the front door, using the key hidden under the mat.

He bent over to get the key and heard a scream across the street.

It was Mrs. Micklemeyer. She had stepped out to get her morning paper. Now she stood with her hands pressed to her cheeks and her eyes bulging out.

Russell slipped inside as fast as he could. Peeking through the window, he saw Mrs. Micklemeyer staring at the house with anger and astonishment on her face.

Well, his parents would know what he had been doing now. Mrs. Micklemeyer never kept her mouth shut.

He tiptoed up the stairway and into his room. His bathrobe hung on the doorknob. He slipped it on.

Inside the room his mother was sitting in the chair beside his bed, sound asleep. Russell knew she had been there all night, waiting for him.

He shook her shoulder softly.

"Mom," he said. "I'm home!"

Her eyes flew open. She jumped up and threw her arms around him, hugging him close.

As he hugged her back, he could feel her tears on his head.

# Epilogue

Russell was sitting in his room, thinking. He was supposed to be doing homework. But thoughts of the ring kept pushing into his mind.

He wasn't sure why. He hadn't thought about it too much once everything had settled down after Halloween week. Of course, there had been a *lot* to settle down.

First he'd had to deal with his parents. He smiled as he remembered the story he had spun out to explain his absence that night.

Actually, it had had bits of truth in it. He had blamed the trouble on the teenage boys, telling his parents they had taken him into the woods and burned his clothes as a Halloween prank. His father had been furious and had wanted to call the police. But Russell had convinced him that there was no point in that, since the boys had been wearing masks and he had no idea who they were.

Then there had been Mr. Rafschnitz and his wall-shaking lecture to Russell on the Monday after Halloween. (Not to mention two weeks of staying after school to pay for his crimes.)

And, of course, there was Eddie. His reaction to Russell in school after Halloween had been so comical that teachers and kids alike had besieged Russell with questions about what had happened. His noncommittal answers had not satisfied them but had left Eddie with some self-respect. Eddie seemed grateful for that.

All because of the ring. He looked at the faint scar it had left on his finger and smiled.

Suddenly he felt a sharp pain there. He looked again, more closely. The scar, usually almost invisible, was bright red. And it was throbbing like it was on fire.

What was going on?

He looked up and saw the moonlight spilling over his windowsill—the light of the first full moon since Halloween.

His skin begin to itch.

His forehead started to throb.

He had a wild urge to howl.

And at last he understood what Mr. Elives had meant by "aftereffects."

He sighed.

"Well, Crannaker," he told himself, "that's what you get for not following directions."

A howl was creeping up his throat. Crossing to the window, he laid a hairy paw on the sill.

It was time to go out for the night.

## About the Author

BRUCE COVILLE was born and raised in upstate New York. He holds a bachelor's degree in elementary education and has taught primary school for a number of years. He has also worked as a salesman, a toymaker, and a grave-digger. Mr. Coville enjoys reading, especially fantasy and mythology; children's theater (he has written two children's musicals, both of which have been produced); and Halloween. Mr. Coville has also written a number of books for children and young adults.

787